Paper Crunch

Karen Rogers and JoAnne Alexander

Contents

Rigby

WAIT!

Don't throw away that piece of paper.

Do you know where that paper comes from? Do you know how much work it took to get that paper into your hand?

Where Does Paper Come From?

It takes a lot of effort to make paper.

It takes time.

It takes trees.

It takes **resources.**

It takes **energy.**

5

Tall, grown trees are cut and taken to **paper mills**.

Mills use lots of energy, like electricity. They use lots of resources, like water. Many run day and night, seven days a week. The mills turn the trees into all different kinds of paper.

Trucks and trains carry the paper
from the mills to stores and factories.
This takes energy, resources, and
time, too.

Do you still want to throw that paper away?
Let's think about where it will go.

Where Does Paper End Up?

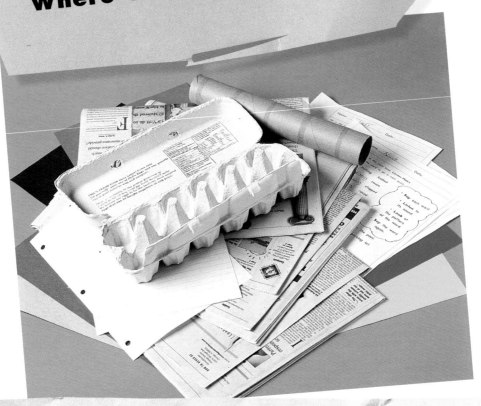

Paper that is thrown away goes to a **landfill**. A landfill is a place where **solid waste** is buried. There are about 15,000 landfills in the United States. They cover large areas of land and get bigger every day.

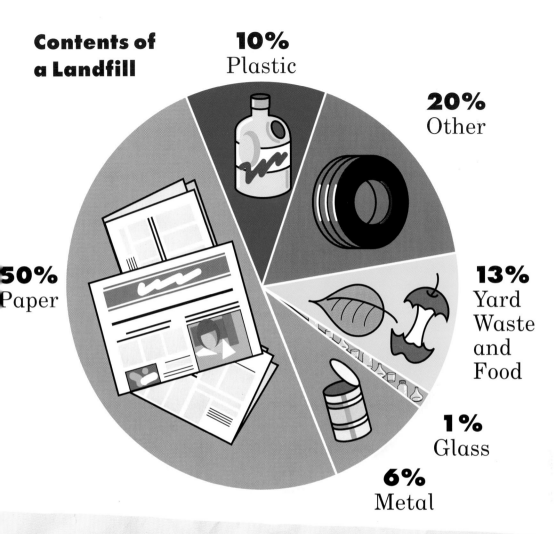

Contents of a Landfill

10% Plastic

20% Other

13% Yard Waste and Food

1% Glass

6% Metal

50% Paper

Paper makes up half of the solid waste in a landfill. So the more paper we throw away, the bigger our landfills get.

Reusing Paper

Maybe you
can reuse
that paper!
You could use it
to help your pets.

Line your bird's cage with it.

Shred it for nesting material for your hamster.

Crinkle it up as a toy for your kitten.

You can use paper to help out around the house. Use paper bags for trash can liners.

Use the funny papers to wrap gifts.

You can reuse paper for arts and crafts.

Make paper bag masks.
Make greeting cards from old calendars.
Make paper chains for party decorations.

Recycling Paper

If you can't reuse that paper, maybe you can **recycle** it!

WE RECYCLE

Recycling paper saves trees. Every ton of paper that is recycled saves 17 trees! Recycling also saves energy and resources. One person recycling paper can make a difference. Lots of people recycling paper can make a big difference.

Set up a place for recycling at home.

Find out where **recycling centers** are located in your area, and encourage your family and neighbors to go there.

Create a place for recycling at school.
Get everyone involved.

WAIT!

Don't throw away that piece of paper. Do you know where that paper comes from?

Glossary

energy power, such as electricity and gas

landfill a place where solid waste is buried

paper mill where paper is produced from wood

recycle to turn waste products into new ones

recycling center a collection place for recyclable materials

resources a source or supply of raw material, such as a tree

solid waste all garbage, trash, and yard waste from homes, factories, and other businesses